DRAGONBREATH
THE FROZEN MENACE

DRAGONBREATH
THE FROZEN MENACE
BY
URSULA VERNON

DIAL BOOKS FOR YOUNG READERS

For my father, who would recite "The Ballad of the Ice-Worm Cocktail" on long car rides

DIAL BOOKS FOR YOUNG READERS
AN IMPRINT OF PENGUIN RANDOM HOUSE, LLC
375 Hudson Street
New York, NY 10014

Library of Congress Cataloging-in-Publication Data
Vernon, Ursula.
  The frozen menace / by Ursula Vernon.
    pages cm. — (Dragonbreath ; 11)
Summary: "Danny Dragonbreath travels to the Farthest North to find a way to relight his fire before it's too late"— Provided by publisher.
  ISBN 978-0-8037-3986-4 (hardcover)
[1. Dragons—Fiction. 2. Adventure and adventurers—Fiction. 3. Humorous stories.] I. Title.
  PZ7.V5985Fr 2016   [Fic]—dc23   2015007669

Printed in the United States of America

10 9 8 7 6 5 4 3 2 1

Design by Jennifer Kelly
Text set in Stempel Schneidler Std

DANNY DRAGONBREATH WAS DRIVING SLED DOGS IN THE IDITAROD.

HE AND HIS TEAM HAD DRIVEN THROUGH BLIZZARDS, THROUGH ICE STORMS, THROUGH SUB-ZERO TEMPERATURES.

IT HAD BEEN NINE GRUELING DAYS OF UNRELENTING SNOW. DANNY WAS GLAD TO BE APPROACHING THE FINISH LINE.

ALSO, HE WAS GETTING VERY TIRED OF STARING AT HUSKY BUTTS.

BUT SUDDENLY, A SNOWSTORM BLEW UP!

He couldn't see the trail.
He couldn't even see the huskies!

If he couldn't find his way to shelter soon, he would freeze to death in the terrible, icy cold . . .

COLD AS ICE

Danny woke up and immediately wished he hadn't.

He'd been dreaming about snow and ice, and when he woke up, it seemed like part of the dream had come with him. There was a frozen knot in his chest that radiated cold.

He pulled the blankets back and poked himself in the chest. His skin felt clammy. The coldness in his chest didn't budge.

"That's weird . . ." said Danny out loud.

He tried to breathe fire. Not a lot of fire—large parts of his room were flammable!—but just a little to get his blood moving.

Nothing happened.

Normally when he was cold, it was easier to breathe fire. He'd had great luck with holding a bag of frozen peas under his chin, although his mom had made him stop because he kept thawing out the peas.

He took a deep breath and thought about things that made him mad—video games that ate your saved game so you had to replay for hours. Big Eddy the school bully. People being mean to animals.

When he exhaled, he breathed frost into the room.

"Whoa," he said.

He slid out of bed and went downstairs.

His father was sitting in the kitchen, reading a book and drinking coffee. He looked up, surprised.

"You're up early, sport. What's wrong?"

I'M COLD. ERR . . . LIKE . . . *REALLY COLD.*

His father frowned. "Are you sick?"

"I might be?" said Danny. This didn't feel like having a fever. It was more like he'd eaten ice cream too fast and chilled his stomach, except instead of warming up, his stomach had gone on to chill his heart and his lungs and his liver and all the other wibbly bits that go into a small dragon's anatomy.

UH—UH—
YOU'RE NOT GONNA
THROW UP, ARE
YOU?

(Danny's father was a "sympathy vomiter," which meant that if someone threw up anywhere near him, Danny's dad would immediately run for the bathroom. Whenever Danny came home sick from school, his father hid in the bedroom until they established that it was a fever and not food poisoning. Danny found the whole thing sort of funny, if tragic.)

"Nah," said Danny. "I'm not queasy. I'm just cold."

Danny's father felt his forehead. "You *feel* cold. I

don't know. I wish your mom were here . . . She'll be back Thursday."

Danny nodded.

"You want to stay home from school?"

"Okay," said Danny, who was not going to turn down a chance to stay home from school. "I'll go back to bed."

"You do that," said his father. As Danny climbed up the stairs to his bedroom, his father called, "You're not allowed to die until Thursday! Your mom will yell at me!"

Danny grinned, despite the cold, and went back to bed.

A RARE DISEASE

He slept for most of the day, and when he woke up, the cold feeling was worse.

His throat felt a bit like when he'd eaten a cough drop and then inhaled deeply, except that it didn't taste like mint. The air hitting the back of his throat was like frost.

It was sort of neat, except for being half-frozen.

He piled blankets on top of himself, and then more blankets, and then a few more. It didn't seem to help. The cold was coming from inside him, not from the air.

He was just thinking of going in search of more blankets when the door opened.

"Wendell!" said Danny happily, sitting up. His best friend, Wendell the iguana, came in, followed by Christiana the crested lizard. "Christiana! What are you guys doing here?"

"We brought you your homework," said Wendell. "Your dad says you're sick."

I GUESS?
I DON'T FEEL SICK.
I'VE JUST GOT THIS WEIRD
COLD SPOT AND I CAN'T
BREATHE FIRE.

YOU CAN'T BREATHE
FIRE *NORMALLY*.

YEAH, BUT AT
LEAST I GET SMOKE
WHEN I TRY! NOW ALL I
GET IS FROST!

"Whoa," said Christiana. "That sounds serious." She frowned at Danny. "I don't really understand the mechanism that lets you breathe fire—I'd probably have to dissect you to figure that out—"

"I'm not that sick!"

"—but that sounds like some kind of weird dragon problem to me." She leaned against the door frame. "Have you asked any dragons?"

"I asked my dad," said Danny. "But he's not really good with medical stuff. I mean, he'll get a headache and Mom will be all 'Did you take some aspirin?' and he's all 'No, I didn't,' and she'll be all 'Why not?' and he'll be like 'I dunno . . .' and—"

FASCINATING AS THIS PLAY-BY-PLAY DISCUSSION OF YOUR FAMILY'S MEDICAL DYSFUNCTION IS, MAYBE YOU SHOULD TALK TO A DOCTOR. A *DRAGON* DOCTOR.

"I don't think there are any," Danny admitted. "We're sort of endangered, and also the total secrecy thing."

"Makes it hard to go to medical school," said Wendell. "What about your granddad? He knows all kinds of stuff. He got that awful wasp out of my dreams that time."

"That's a great idea!" said Danny. He draped himself in blankets and led the procession downstairs to the phone.

The phone rang eighteen times, which was pretty normal for Danny's grandfather. Then it was picked up and Danny heard: "Eh? What? Is this thing on?"

"IT'S ME, GREAT-GRANDDAD!" yelled Danny into the receiver.

"Eh? You're not my granddad! My granddad was swallowed by the Great Toad of Prosperity and became immortal, for all the good it does him inside a toad. Unless you mean my granddad on my mother's side—"

"NO!" yelled Danny. "You're MY great-granddad! It's Danny!"

"Oh, right, right. How are you, boy?"

I THINK I'M SICK, GRANDDAD . . .

He explained—loudly—the strange cold sensation he'd been feeling.

"Now that's interesting . . ."

"He says it's interesting," said Danny to Wendell and Christiana.

"Good interesting?" asked Wendell. "Or 'Wow, you've got a disease so rare that they're going to name it after you' interesting?"

"That'd be kind of neat," said Danny. "Danny's Reverse Fever! I'll be famous!"

"I always figured you'd end up in a medical textbook one way or another . . ." muttered Christiana.

ARE YOU WELL ENOUGH TO TRAVEL?

"I think so," said Danny. "I mean, it doesn't hurt, it's just weird."

"Come out and see me," said Great-Grandfather Dragonbreath. "It could be serious, and if it is, there's no time to lose." He considered. "And bring that little friend of yours out too. Wanda, was it?"

"Wendell . . ." said Danny, but his great-grandfather had already hung up the phone.

TO THE BUS!

"Are you sure you want to come with me?" asked Danny as they left the house. He'd written a note to his dad saying that he was going to Great-Granddad's house and that Wendell and Christiana were with him.

"I don't really mind being called Wanda," said Wendell. "I'm kind of used to it. And I like your great-granddad."

"It's not that," said Danny. "It's . . . well . . . I'm sick. Sort of. Aren't you afraid you'll catch it?"

"Honestly, I was surprised you agreed to come

along and give him his homework," said Christiana. "I know how you are about germs."

Wendell squirmed. "Yeah," he said. "Okay, I'm a little worried."

BUT YOU'RE MY BEST FRIEND. AND I BROUGHT LOTS AND LOTS AND *LOTS* OF HAND SANITIZER.

He opened his backpack, revealing a large jug.

"That may be overkill," said Christiana. "Or at least a fire hazard."

"If worse comes to worst, you can always bathe in it," said Danny. "Anyway, this is probably a dragon-specific sort of problem. It probably won't do anything to iguanas."

"Right," said Wendell, sounding not very convinced.

Danny noticed that the iguana was careful to keep Christiana between them, but he didn't say anything. It was already pretty brave of Wendell to come along at all.

They got on the bus. The bus driver raised an eyebrow at Danny's blanket-covered attire, but said nothing.

"So where does your great-granddad live?" asked Christiana.

"Mythical Japan," said Danny.

There was a long pause.

MYTHICAL JAPAN.

"Yup," said Danny.
They waited.
Christiana nodded once. "All right, then."

"Anyway," said Christiana, "skepticism isn't about disbelieving everything, it's about disbelieving stuff that doesn't have proof. And I've got plenty of proof that very *weird* things happen around you. One of these days, I'll figure out how it works."

Danny had to admit that it was easier to live with Christiana when she wasn't denying that he was really a dragon, but he did kind of miss being able to tease her about it.

He rubbed his chest. The cold felt sharper. He pulled the blankets more tightly around his shoulders.

It took a transfer, but the bus driver finally called: "Next stop, mythical Japan!" Wendell reached up and pulled the cord to request a stop.

"What I'd like to know," said Christiana as they all piled off the bus, "is whether or not the bus drivers remember these stops, or whether it's some kind of weird dragon magic."

"It's just a good bus system," said Danny.

Mythical Japan looked like it usually did—snow and bamboo and ancient, gnarled trees. Danny's grandfather lived on the outskirts in a small, tastefully appointed house surrounded by trees, hot springs, and his greenhouse.

"Wow," said Christiana, looking around. "This looks like a Hokusai painting."

"Who?" asked Danny.

"Hokusai. Great Japanese painter in the Edo period."

". . . okay," said Danny.

"If your great-granddad lives here, I think Hokusai's technically part of your cultural heritage," said Christiana.

"Neat!" said Danny.

". . . Philistine," muttered Christiana.

"Was he a painter too?"

Wendell snickered. "It means somebody who doesn't know about culture," he told Danny. Danny rolled his eyes.

It was a short walk through the bamboo thickets to Danny's great-grandfather's house. Snow lay more thickly than usual on everything. It crunched underfoot as they walked.

"Wonder if Suki will be here . . ." said Wendell.

"Aw, man," said Christiana. "I haven't seen her in ages! How is she?" (Suki the exchange student lived in the real-world Japan, but visited mythical Japan occasionally, which was where Danny and Wendell usually ran into her.)

"She's fine," said Wendell. "We saw her just the other—Danny!?"

26

Danny, much to his own surprise, had collapsed in a heap in the snow.

Christiana and Wendell both took an arm and pulled him to his feet.

"Are you okay?" asked Wendell. "Do you feel weak?"

"No," said Danny. "Just cold."

The snow underfoot had been chilling his toes, sure—not badly, just enough to be felt through the thick scales on his feet. But then his chest had given a strange pulse of coldness in response, and suddenly the world had tilted sideways and he had pitched over into a snowdrift.

Christiana slung an arm over his shoulders. "Come on," she said. "I'll help you. Jeez! You're like a block of ice!" She shifted her weight. "How close is this place?"

"It's close," said Wendell, slathering hand sanitizer on his fingers.

"I'm fine," said Danny. "I don't know what happened. It was actually kind of neat, things went all *swooooosh* sideways and then I fell over!"

"Yeah," said Christiana. "Neat. And the bit where you die of hypothermia will be totally awesome too, I'm sure."

"I'd rather die of hypothermia than sarcasm," muttered Danny, but allowed Christiana to help him through the snow.

EXTINGUISHED

When they reached Danny's great-granddad's house, Wendell ran ahead to the door and hammered on it.

Normally it took a few minutes for the elderly dragon to make his way to the door, but this time it opened immediately.

"Wanda!" said Great-Grandfather Dragon-breath. "You made it! Where's Danny?"

"Right behind me, sir," said Wendell. "He fell over in the snow. I think there's something really wrong."

The old dragon scowled, and his long catfish whiskers twitched. "That's bad," he said. "I was hoping it would just be a minor ailment, but it sounds like a full extinguishing."

"A what?"

Grandfather Dragonbreath pushed past him and hurried down the path. He scooped Danny up in his arms.

"That's probably why you're still alive," said his great-grandfather. "I can tell just by touching you that you're chilled to the bone."

"I'm cold," Danny admitted as he was carried into the house, "but it's more like I've got cold *in* me, not like I *feel* cold, if that makes any sense . . ."

"It makes a great deal of sense," said his great-grandfather grimly. He plopped Danny down on the couch inside the house and turned to Danny's friends.

FORGIVE ME, YOUNG LADY, FOR NOT GREETING YOU SOONER. THANK YOU FOR HELPING MY GRANDSON.

Danny was a little surprised that Christiana did not explode at being called "young lady." Normally she would have delivered a lengthy tirade about how she wasn't a lady and then followed it up with something about oppressive gender roles.

"Are you sure *you're* not sick?" Danny asked.

Christiana rolled her eyes. "I'll make allowances for the older generation," she muttered. "Particularly since you're, I dunno, *currently dying*."

"Can you fix him, sir?" asked Wendell worriedly.

"Temporarily," said Grandfather Dragonbreath. "You, Danny—stay there and don't move a muscle. Wanda, young lady—come with me."

"It's Christiana," said Christiana, following the elderly dragon toward the kitchen.

"Eh? Don't mumble, now. Speak up!"

CHRISTIANA!

DON'T HAVE TO SHOUT. YOU CAN CALL ME GRANDFATHER. EVERYBODY DOES.

They went into the kitchen. Danny lay on the couch, feeling a little left out.

He thought about getting up, but then he noticed his toes.

They were turning pale green—not a healthy lizard green, but the cold color at the heart of a glacier. There were hints of blue around the edges.

He tried to wiggle them. Nothing happened.

He poked one with his fingers. It felt cold and numb.

Danny started to think that maybe this was serious after all.

His grandfather came out of the kitchen, carrying a tray with tea steaming on it.

"What's happening?" asked Danny. Frost came out of his mouth when he talked.

"Simple," said his grandfather. "I'm afraid your fire's gone out."

THE MAGICAL REFRIGERATOR

"My fire? Really? That can happen?"

"Occasionally," said Great-Grandfather. "Only to fire-breathing dragons, of course." He thumped his own chest. "You get that from your grandmother's side of the family. My side of the family are mostly water-dragons. Water doesn't go out, but it can dry up—well, anyway. Neither here nor there! You get a cold and it gets into your lungs and instead of pneumonia, your fire goes out. Saw it happen to your great-uncle once, and made up a treatment."

He poured out some tea and handed Danny a cup.

"I had a cold two weeks ago . . ." said Danny. "I thought I was over it."

"There you are, then."

The tea smelled very strange. Danny drank it anyway.

It tasted . . . *hot.*

"What is it?"

"Ginger and peppermint, cayenne and chamomile." The elderly dragon held up a finger. "And a very large dollop of fireweed honey."

"Fireweed?" asked Danny. "That sounds cool! Is it on fire?"

"In the mythical world it is," said Great-Grandfather. "Burns like anything. The bees have to wear flame-retardant vests. In your world, it's a bit more tame."

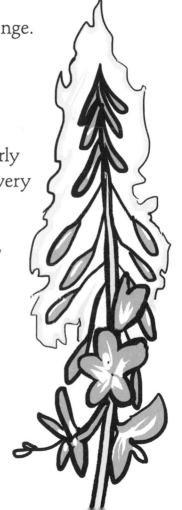

"I think my mom grows it in her garden," said Wendell. "It's pink, though, and it doesn't burn."

"Well, that's only to be expected out in the regular world," said Great-Grandfather, refilling Danny's teacup. "You can't get the vests, for one thing. The honey is still pretty good, but it won't put fire inside you the way the mythical stuff does."

Christiana sat on the couch, practically vibrating with the desire to yell about all of these things being completely and totally impossible, but said nothing. Danny was impressed by her restraint.

> NOT A CHANCE!

". . . oh."

Danny took another sip. The coldness in his feet receded. The strange cold knot was still there, but it seemed like there was a warm barrier around it now, keeping it in.

"I feel like one of those candies," he said. "It's all cold and minty in the middle, but the tea is making kind of a chocolate shell."

Great-Grandfather grinned. "Well, I could give you a lot of talk about energy and chi, but that's as good an explanation as any."

He began pouring tea into a thermos. "You'll need to keep drinking it," he said. "Until you get your fire relit."

BUT HOW DO I GET MY FIRE RELIT?

OH, THAT'S SIMPLE. YOU'LL NEED TO SWALLOW SOME PHOENIX EGGSHELLS. SHOULD START THINGS RIGHT BACK UP.

GREAT!

WHERE DO
WE GET PHOENIX
EGGSHELLS?

Great-Grandfather Dragonbreath tapped his snout. "There you go, Wanda, always asking the good questions. The answer is that you get them from a phoenix nest. Just don't swallow the baby phoenix with it, that's not cool."

Christiana listened to this without saying anything, although she had an expression of deep disbelief.

"I used to keep eggshell around, but it's hard to get," said Great-Grandfather. "Used the last of it on your great-uncle, as it happens, which is how I know it works."

"So where do we find a phoenix?" asked Danny.

"In the Farthest North. Just before the End of the World. If you reach the End of the World, you've gone too far, turn around."

"You mean like the North Pole?" asked Wendell.

"That's up there too, probably. Anyway, you go to the Farthest North and you look up and the phoenixes will be dancing in the sky. They live up there because they're too hot. If they come too far south, they'll burn up."

Christiana's expression of disbelief deepened.

Danny stood up. The room didn't whoosh sideways or anything. This was a great improvement.

"Will it be dangerous?" asked Wendell.

OH, YEAH, HORRIBLY PERILOUS, FEROCIOUS ICEWORMS, BITING COLD, ALL THAT GOOD STUFF.

He handed around cups of the fireweed tea. "Drink that up, it'll keep you from freezing to death. Mostly."

Christiana sipped her tea and grimaced. Wendell drank his down without flinching.

"What?" he said, when she stared at him. "It's no worse than the herbal stuff my mom makes. That has, like, brewer's yeast and St. John's wort and stuff."

"Finish your tea," said Great-Grandfather Dragonbreath. "Then we'll send you off to the Farthest North."

AND JUST HOW ARE WE GETTING TO THIS "FARTHEST NORTH"?

MAGICAL PORTAL IN THE REFRIGERATOR.

"I don't believe in magic," said Christiana, scowling.

"Very sensible," said Great-Grandfather Dragonbreath. "Believing in it only encourages it." He handed Danny the thermos of tea.

"I will admit that Danny can do some interesting things with the bus system," said Christiana, "but I'm sure there's a logical explanation."

"Absolutely there is," said the old dragon. "And the logical explanation is magic. But I still wouldn't go believing in it. You might want to close your eyes going through the portal, though."

"I went through the portal once to get into Wendell's dreams!" said Danny cheerfully. "It was SO cool!"

"Not for me," said Wendell. "There was a horrible giant wasp laying eggs and . . ." He shuddered.

They walked into the kitchen and Danny's grandfather opened the refrigerator door.

Danny glanced at Christiana. She stared at the swirling energy inside the fridge and narrowed her eyes.

"You don't *have* to go . . ." he began.

She snorted loudly. "No scientist, given a chance to experience something beyond her understanding, would pass up the chance. At least, no scientist *I'd* want to be."

She walked into the portal. Wendell followed.

"You've got good friends, grandson," said Great-Grandfather Dragonbreath. "I approve of them." He patted Danny on the shoulder. "When you eat the eggshell, you might find that things get a little . . . err . . . overheated. You'll be in the Farthest North, so there won't be anything to burn down, but try to aim away from your buddies."

"I will, Great-Granddad. Thanks." Danny hugged the old dragon, then followed his friends into the swirling lights of the portal.

THE EXPEDITION BEGINS

The Farthest North was black and white.

The snow was white and the sky was black. The stars were white and the stones were black and all the shadows were as sharp as knives.

"Whoa," said Danny.

The portal had spit them out on a small rise. The wall behind them was a sheet of ice.

"Is anyone else bothered by the fact that we can't get back?" asked Christiana.

"It'll reopen when we've got the eggshell," said Danny confidently, not because he knew that for certain but because it seemed like the sort of thing a magical portal would do.

"What if we don't get the eggshell?" asked Wendell. "Will we have to stay here forever? What will we eat?"

"Each other," said Christiana. "All good Arctic expeditions eventually devolve into cannibalism."

"We'll eat Wendell," said Danny. "His mom feeds him health food all day. He's gotta be, like, super-healthy."

"HEY!"

Wendell gave them both a worried look and absently began washing with hand sanitizer.

"So where's this phoenix we're supposed to find?" asked Christiana.

"Dunno," said Danny. "I guess we just wander around 'til we find one . . ."

Christiana looked from him to the vast snow-field, back to him, and back to the snowfield. "Sure," she said. "That sounds totally productive."

Far overhead, against the roof of stars, a white point of light went streaking across the sky.

WHAT'S THAT?

"Comet?" said Christiana. "Aurora?"

The light zipped sideways, up and down, rolling and swooping. It seemed to come closer and, for a moment, Danny thought he saw wings.

"That must be the phoenix!" he said. "Follow it!"

"It could be hundreds of miles away!" said Christiana. "We don't even know if it's . . . oh, never mind."

Danny was already hurrying down the slope. He left long skidding footprints in the snow.

The dot of light cut an elaborate figure eight in the sky, then dove down below the horizon.

"It must be in those mountains!" said Danny. "We just have to get there!"

Wendell rubbed the back of his neck.

THEY LOOK AWFULLY FAR AWAY . . .

"We'll just have to hope there's a lot of ice crystals in the air, contributing to the atmospheric perspective," said Christiana.

"Yeah, that," said Danny. "C'mon!"

He led the way into the Farthest North.

OVER THE EDGE

At the bottom of the slope, there were two poles about three feet high. A rope hung between them, and on the rope hung a sign that creaked in the wind.

The trio stopped in front of it.

"FARTHEST NORTH," Wendell read aloud. "PROCEED WITH CAUTION. NO LIFEGUARD ON DUTY."

They looked around.

"Why would you need a lifeguard?" asked Danny. "You can't go swimming."

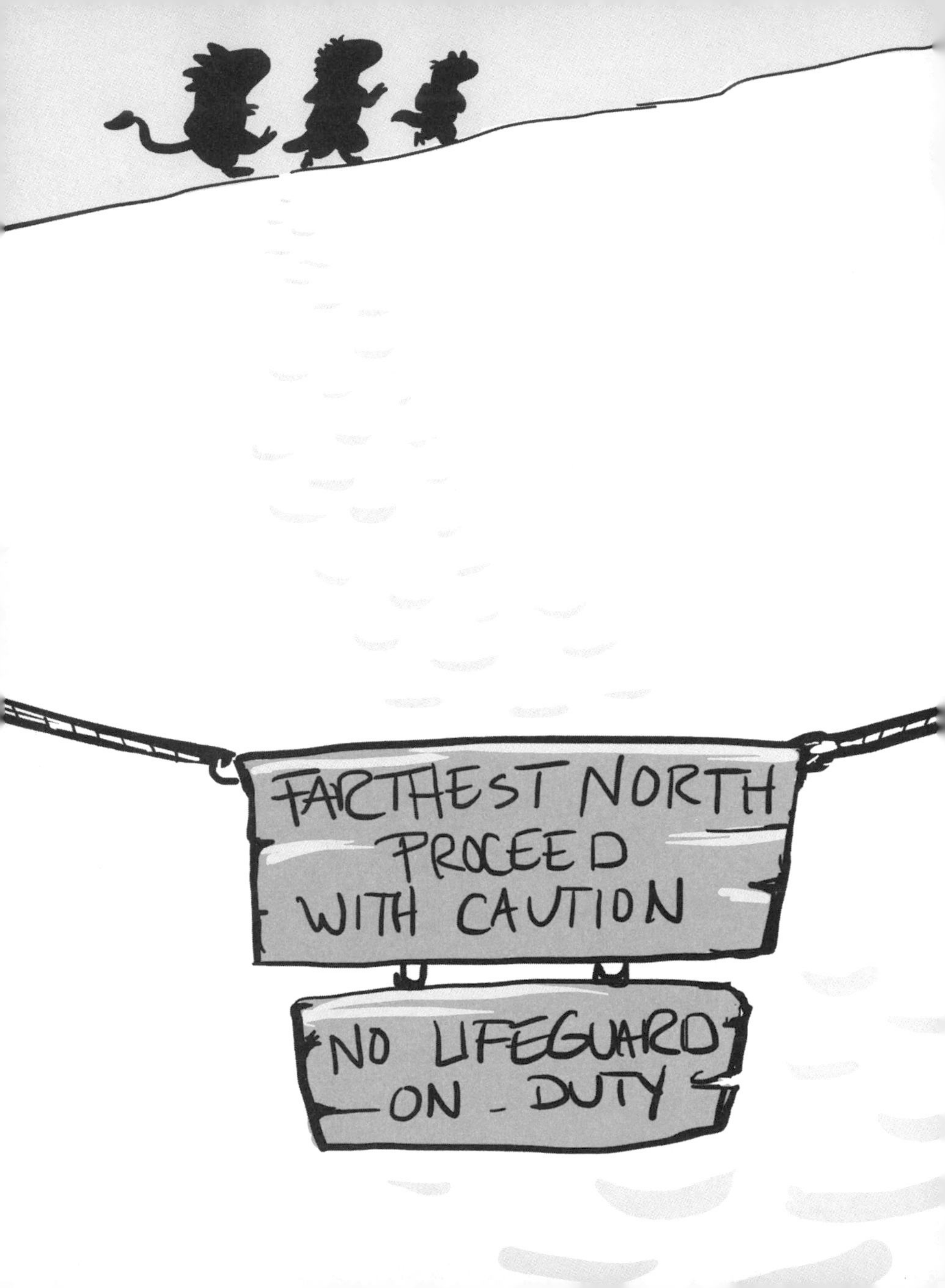
FARTHEST NORTH
PROCEED
WITH CAUTION
NO LIFEGUARD
ON DUTY

"Maybe they're preparing for global warming," muttered Christiana.

The wind blew, the sign creaked, and that was all. Danny looked back over at the mountains to get his bearings. The phoenix had gone to earth near a set of tall stones that looked a bit like a sleeping frog.

They started walking.

"How are you feeling, Danny?" asked Wendell.

"I feel okay." Danny took another sip of tea from the thermos. The coldness in his chest seemed a bit sharper, probably in response to all the snow, but the heat from the tea drove it back. He screwed the lid on tightly. If he collapsed in the middle of all this snow, he'd be an icicle in minutes. "How are you guys?"

"I ought to be freezing to death, but I feel okay," said Christiana. "Which is either a miracle or that stage of hypothermia where you start to feel hot."

"You start to feel hot?" asked Danny.

"Yeah, when somebody's freezing, sometimes

they feel overheated. Lots of people take off their coats and roll around in snow because they're burning up. It's called 'paradoxical undressing.'"

"Neat!" said Danny. "Then what happens?"

"They die."

THAT'S . . . LESS NEAT . . . ?

"It takes a super-long time, though," said Wendell. "And if you're freezing, sometimes they can warm you up and you don't actually die." The iguana struck a pose. "Doctors like to say you're not *really* dead until you're *warm* and dead."

Trust Wendell to know all about it, thought Danny. If there was any horrible medical condition you could experience, the iguana was an expert.

Death probably counted as a medical condition, right?

"Anyway, I'm going with 'miracle,'" said Christiana. "And when we get back to civilization, I want to analyze that tea."

"If there's any left, it's all yours," said Danny.

They had been walking through the snow for only a few minutes when they saw another sign up ahead.

"Who knew the Farthest North would have so many signs?" asked Wendell.

This one was also hanging between two poles, and it read WARNING: BOTTOMLESS CHASM AHEAD.

In smaller letters underneath, it said NO FISHING FROM BRIDGE.

"If it's really a bottomless chasm, where would the fish be?" asked Wendell.

"I guess that's why there's no fishing," said Danny.

"So, this is bad," said Christiana, pointing.

They looked at the bridge.

It was narrow and snow-covered and white. It was impossible to tell if it was solid or if it was made entirely of snow and ice.

They looked at the bridge some more. It did not get any wider or any more sturdy looking.

"I don't wanna cross that," said Wendell.

"I think we have to," said Danny. "C'mon, it can't be that bad. They wouldn't put up a sign if it was just made of snow . . ."

"Yeah, but what if it's snow over ice?" said Wendell. "You could take a step and your feet would go out from under you and *whoosh!* Right into the bottomless chasm! You'd fall forever and ever and ever."

Danny frowned.

Christiana looked from him to the bridge to Wendell and said, "Hmm."

"Hmm?" asked Danny. "What do you mean, hmm?"

"How much do you weigh?" asked Christiana.

"Seventy-seven pounds," said Danny.

"Right," said Christiana. "Then we'll send you first."

She went to the sign and unhooked the rope from one of the poles.

"Aren't they going to yell at us for taking down their sign?" asked Wendell worriedly, as if this small act of vandalism would instantly summon an angry adult.

"Not as much as your mom will yell if we let you fall into a bottomless pit," said Danny.

"Okay," said Christiana. "Here's the deal. Danny goes first 'cos he's heaviest. Tie the rope around your waist, and if you fall, the other end is tied to the pole and you won't fall forever and we can pull you up. When you're on the other side, unhook the rope and we'll pull it back. I'll go second, and then Wendell last."

Danny was a little annoyed that Christiana was giving orders—this was, after all, *his* quest to find a phoenix to relight *his* fire, but he had to admit that it was a pretty good plan.

He hooked the rope in a crude harness under his arms and began inching his way across the bridge.

The wind came up before he had gone more than a few feet. He had to lean against the wind and set his feet very carefully. Each foot had to be flat and solid and not slide even the teensiest bit.

He was a bit surprised when he made it across and dropped to his knees in the snow.

Oh man, he thought, Wendell is gonna *hate* that.

The far side of the chasm was rockier, with tall boulders covered in snow. Danny looked out across the snowfield and thought it seemed lumpier, but it was hard to tell. Everything was so white.

He unhooked the rope and dropped it. Christiana began to pull it back across the gap.

Wendell put his hands up to his mouth and called, "How bad is it?"

NOT AS BAD AS IT LOOKS!

Christiana tied the rope around herself and set out across the bridge. She wobbled a few times as the wind hit her, and her jacket billowed, but she made it across in short order and collapsed next to Danny.

"Okay," she said. "That was actually pretty awful."

"Don't tell Wendell that," Danny muttered. "I don't want to leave him there while we go off looking for eggshells."

Christiana straightened up. Wendell untied the other end from the pole and looped it around himself.

"What's he doing?" asked Danny.

"Oh," said Christiana. "That's actually a better idea than mine. This way, if he falls in, we can pull him up. Otherwise he'd be hanging off the cliff and we'd have to go back across the bridge to get to him."

She passed Danny the far end of the rope and wrapped the middle around herself. They both braced themselves.

Wendell stood indecisively on the far end of the bridge. He took a step out and the wind blew and he froze.

"You can do it, Wendell!" called Christiana. Under her breath, she said, "He's not going to do it."

"He will," said Danny. "Wendell may act like a big chicken, but he always comes through in the end." Out loud he yelled, "C'mon, Wendell! It's not any worse than the time we climbed that castle!"

"I hated climbing that castle!" Wendell shouted back, but he took a few more steps out onto the bridge.

"And it's not nearly as bad as when you had to crawl into the giant bat cave!"

"And remember the time we were dangled over a live volcano!"

"I hated that volcano, but at least it was warm!"

Christiana cupped her hands around her mouth. "Hey, remember that hallway full of evil clown ghosts? This is way less scary!"

"I hated that hallway!" shouted Wendell, who was by now at the halfway point on the bridge. "And I think I'm going to get different friends who aren't always dragging me on horrible adventures where I am in danger of being killed by ghosts or bats or clowns or falling from a great height!"

"Shoulda done that before we went through the portal!" called Christiana. Danny rolled his eyes.

"I want off this bridge!" cried Wendell, and then the wind blew him off his feet and into the bottomless chasm.

ICEWORMS AND FIERY BIRDS

Christiana yelped, and then yelped again as Wendell's weight hit the end of the rope. She was dragged a few feet toward the cliff edge before she managed to slow down, bracing her feet in the snow.

Unfortunately, snow skids. She tried to walk backward, but every time she planted her feet, she slipped.

Danny hurried to take some of the weight off. He looked around and saw a boulder.

"Hold on!" he yelled.

It was hard going. Who would have thought that the iguana weighed so much? Every time Danny took a step, he was nearly yanked off his feet.

Danny shot a glance over his shoulder and saw Christiana nearly at the cliff edge. If she went over, they were all going to fall. There was no way that Danny could take their combined weight all on his shoulders.

"Hold on!" he said again.

"I'm trying!" snapped Christiana.

Danny grabbed for the boulder and got his hands on it. It was too large and icy to get a grip. He was going to have to walk around it with the rope. He didn't know if he had enough rope to *do* that. It was pulled agonizingly tight and was cutting into his scales under his shirt.

Christiana was practically at the edge of the chasm now.

"I need a little more rope!" croaked Danny. He hoped that Christiana had heard him. He could hardly breathe with the rope around his chest like that.

ALMOST . . . GOT IT . . . NEED . . . MORE. . . .

Christiana took a deep breath, nodded—and fell over backward.

Danny got a precious few inches of slack and threw himself at the boulder. Christiana's tail went over the edge.

She teetered for a moment . . . a moment more . . .

And nothing happened. She didn't fall over the edge.

Danny, crammed into a crack in the stone, breathed a long sigh of relief. The terrible pressure of the rope had eased.

The boulder was taking most of the weight now. All he had to do was cling to it and not let go.

"Is Wendell okay?" Danny yelled. "I can't see him!"

"I'll look!" Christiana slowly climbed to her feet. "Wendell?" she called. "Wendell, are you okay down there?"

For a long moment, there was no reply.

Danny tensed.

Had the rope come undone?

Danny sagged against the stone, feeling limp with relief.

"Try to get your feet against the wall," said Christiana. "You can walk up it as I walk back. Ready?"

"Ready!" called the iguana.

Slowly, one step at a time, Christiana walked

backward. Danny hurried to take up the slack. The rope slid over the boulder and he tried not to think about fraying or breaking or any of the calamities that could happen to rather questionable ropes in the middle of the Farthest North.

The rope stopped sliding and began to jerk back and forth. Danny poked his head around the edge of the boulder.

"I'm alive," said Wendell, and burst into tears.

The iguana's breakdown only lasted for a moment. Danny pretended he was very busy with the rope, while Christiana slapped Wendell on the back. "You did fine," she said. "We're all okay."

"I will never be okay again," said Wendell, wiping his eyes.

"You weren't okay to begin with," said Danny cheerfully.

Wendell glared at him. "It's a good thing you just saved my life," he grumbled.

"Or what?" asked Danny.

"Or this!" said Wendell, and threw a snowball into his face.

OH YEAH!?

TAKE THAT!

PFFF! IS THAT THE BEST YOU'VE GOT? YOU THROW LIKE A GIRL!

"Thought so," said Christiana. She looped the rope over her shoulder while Danny and Wendell brushed snow out of their eyes. Wendell dumped hand sanitizer over himself, presumably to guard against tainted snowballs.

Danny took another sip of the fireweed tea. "Okay," he said. "Let's get going."

They set out across the snowfield.

Another sign appeared in the distance.

"What do you think this one says?" asked Wendell.

"Probably no loitering," said Danny, who had been told to stop loitering outside the comic shop just last week. (He had tried to explain that he wasn't loitering, he was just standing there doing nothing, but they had been very grumpy about the whole thing.)

"We're not loitering," said Christiana. "We're walking very quickly, given how snowy it is."

They reached the sign.

"Iceworm?" said Danny. "What's an iceworm? Are they like earthworms?"

"You'd think a worm would have a really hard time in frozen ground," said Christiana. "I mean, they dig through dirt . . ."

"Actually, there's a type of worm that lives on glaciers," said Wendell. *"Mesenchytraeus solifugus."*

"It's not so much that you knew that as that you knew how to *pronounce* it," said Danny.

Wendell looked smug.

THE NOBLE GLACIER ICEWORM
MESENCHYTRAEUS SOLIFUGUS

LOOKS LIKE A WORM.
ACTS LIKE A WORM.
PRETTY DARN WORM-LIKE.

← *1/4 THE SIZE OF A DIME!*

77

"Are they carnivores?" asked Christiana.

"Nah," said Wendell, stepping confidently out into the iceworm preserve. "They're teeny. Less than an inch long. They eat algae."

The ground grew more uneven as they walked, covered in humps and hummocks of snow that might be hiding rocks or boulders or houses or full-size city buses.

Danny got to the top of a small rise and let out a whoop.

"Look!" he cried, pointing. "Look! It's the phoenix!"

Wendell and Christiana looked up.

The phoenix shot overhead like a comet, trailing flames. It was blindingly white, but white with colors around the edges—blues and greens, like the hottest part of a flame.

It was eerily silent as it passed. Danny could hear a very faint whistling, but that might have been the wind.

The aurora flared up behind it, pulsing green and brilliant. "Northern lights!" said Wendell, delighted.

"They're just solar radiation interacting with the atmosphere," said Christiana. "Aurora borealis. It's the phoenix that gets me! It looks like a bird . . ."

"A really *big* bird," said Wendell. "Do you think it's dangerous?"

"Well, mythologically, they set fire to themselves and then rise again from the ashes, right?" said Danny. "So I guess they could probably give you a pretty good burn."

"That doesn't seem like a very good way of maintaining a viable population," said Christiana. "I mean, what if it has an accident?"

"I guess that's why they lay eggs," said Wendell. "So that there's another one around in case it has an accident and can't turn to ashes."

The phoenix, unconcerned by accidents, flew downward, into a set of boulders. Light shattered off the snow around it, then settled.

"Thataway!" cried Danny, pointing.

He started to run.

At the same moment, Wendell started to scream.

WHEN ICEWORMS
GET MAD . . .

Danny heard the iguana shrick and slowed. Had he fallen into another pit? (Really, you couldn't take Wendell anywhere. If it wasn't falling into chasms, it was something else . . .)

The dragon turned.

Underneath Wendell's feet, the snow was moving.

"Help!" cried Wendell. "Help! Earthquake! Snowquake! Help!"

Christiana was floundering toward him, but snow was rolling down the slope onto her and she slid back as quickly as she climbed.

"What *is* that?" said Danny. He turned his back on the phoenix and ran back toward the iguana.

The ground rose and rose until it was taller than Danny, taller than the surrounding boulders, taller than a two-story building. Wendell flung himself flat.

"Crud!" said Christiana. "I think it's an ice-worm!"

"I thought they were teeny!" said Danny.

"I don't think it knows that!"

The iceworm was enormous. It looked like a massive white earthworm, with a greenish head. Danny couldn't see eyes or anything like them, only a lipless mouth and thick rings.

The iceworm shook itself. Snow flew. So did Wendell.

The iguana sailed through the air and landed in a snowdrift. Danny and Christiana ran toward him.

"Do you think it can see us?" asked Danny.

"I don't want to find out!"

The monster bent its segmented head down toward Wendell.

He kicked out wildly and booted the iceworm on the snout.

It recoiled. Danny dashed to Wendell's side and pulled him upright. "I think you hurt it!" he said.

The iceworm opened its mouth and roared.

The sound was strange and guttural, like a lion roaring through a very long drainpipe.

"I think I made it mad . . ." said Wendell.

"Them," said Christiana.

"What?"

She pointed. "Them. You made *them* mad."

All across the snowfield, the giant hummocks of snow were coming to life.

RUN!

They ran. Around them, iceworms erupted from under the snow. It was like being surrounded by vengeful mile-long spaghetti.

"Iceworm preserve," gasped Wendell. "Who's going to preserve *us* from the iceworms?"

"Get to the rocks!" said Danny. "If we can get up on the rocks, we won't be stepping on them!"

This was easier said than done. It was impossible to tell what was rock and what was an iceworm. They were halfway up a hillside when it began to shudder under them. Christiana and Danny had to grab Wendell under the arms to keep him from sliding back down.

"Jump!" shouted Danny, and did.

"Are they following us?" panted Christiana as the great green heads of the iceworms turned toward them. Another one roared and then another. The air filled with the hollow sounds of raging worms.

"Iceworms are blind!" said Wendell. "They can't see us!"

"*Earthworms* are very sensitive to vibrations, though," said Christiana. "These can probably hear our footsteps."

"So how do we stop that?" asked Danny, not slowing down. As he watched, another iceworm turned toward them and began to undulate in their direction.

"Walk without rhythm," said Wendell miserably.

Danny tried hopping on one foot and then zigzagging. This slowed him down, but the iceworms kept coming.

"I don't think it's working!"

The blunt head of an iceworm slammed down beside them. Christiana flung herself sideways, narrowly missing getting flattened.

"Are you sure they eat algae?!" she snapped.

"Maybe they have giant scary algae here!"

The iceworm lifted its head and doubled back on itself, sniffing along its own length as if expecting to find Christiana squished there.

"I don't think they're very smart!" called Danny.

THEY DON'T HAVE TO BE SMART, THEY'RE GIGANTIC!

Another iceworm crashed down over the top of the first. The first one roared in outrage.

"Maybe if we stood absolutely still—" Christiana began.

Danny launched himself at her and knocked her out of the way as a third iceworm popped up from the snow practically at their feet.

"Or we could just run," said Danny.

"Let's do that."

The rocks looked tantalizingly close. They ran toward them. Danny's neck ached from trying to look in all directions at once. He could hear the *sluff-sluff-sluff* sound of the snow dragging against the bodies of the worms.

Wendell started to fall behind and Danny grabbed his arm.

"Just a little farther . . ." he panted.

"I don't know if I can go a little farther," gasped Wendell.

And then the ground under their feet moved as the biggest iceworm of all breached from underneath the snow.

WORM FOOD

It was bigger than a bus, bigger than a semi-trailer, bigger than anything had any right to be. The only thing Danny could think of that had been the same size was the giant squid he had encountered years ago, far down in the ocean depths.

The three kids were at one edge of the worm's back and rolled right off. Danny stayed more or less upright, surfing down the falling snow—Wendell didn't even try. They landed in a heap together, with the iceworm's back like a wall of white flesh beside them.

The worm turned. Its blunt, eyeless head hung suspended in the air over them.

"Don't . . . move . . ." whispered Christiana.

The wall of flesh flexed beside them. It was disgusting on a massive scale.

The head dipped lower. Danny wondered if it could feel them breathing. He held his breath.

Slowly, slowly, it swung toward him. If it had eyes, he'd be staring into them.

It wouldn't have to eat him. All it would have to do is push down and Danny would be squished into the snow like a . . .

Well, like an earthworm.

Wendell whimpered and Christiana shushed him.

The worm's mouth opened over his head.

Danny found himself staring at the inside of the worm. It looked a great deal like the outside of the iceworm—cold and fleshy and made of rings.

It's going to eat me, Danny thought. That's not going to be good. I don't think it can chew, but I don't want to find out.

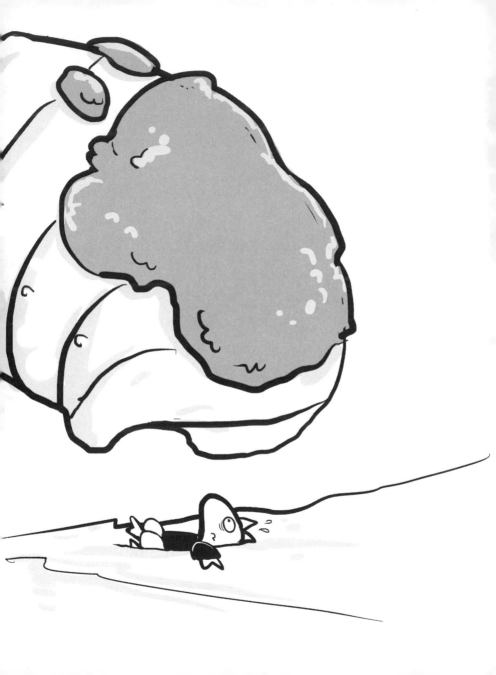

If I could breathe fire, I could torch it right now.

If I could breathe fire, I wouldn't be here in the first place!

The iceworm plunged downward, taking an enormous bite of snow, dirt, and Danny. Everything went dark. Danny felt himself lifted into the air.

It probably didn't matter if he made any vibrations now, so—"Put me down!" Danny yelled into the dark as the worm swallowed him.

Then his nose filled with the scent of burning and the worm screamed.

Danny rolled through the snow, tried to get to his feet, and staggered. For a moment he wasn't sure which way was up and tried to stand sideways.

When he got his head and his tail sorted out, he looked up and saw the phoenix flying low over the snowfield.

As he watched, it dove at the iceworm. It was significantly smaller than the worm was, but the fire pouring off its wings scorched the worm's back. The worm roared.

"The phoenix burned the worm and it spit me out . . ." said Danny, half to himself.

He made for the rocks. His head was ringing from his landing in the snow, and the coldness in his chest was back and worse than ever.

Ahead, he could see Christiana and Wendell. They had made it to the shelter of the stones and were waving frantically to him.

The phoenix blazed past him. The fire felt wonderfully warm. He needed another drink of fireweed tea, but he didn't dare stop.

He looked toward the rocks again. Wendell and Christiana weren't waving anymore, they were . . . pointing? And shouting?

He turned his head.

The iceworm that had come up beside him was smaller than the giant one—only the size of a couple of cars stuck together. Perhaps it was smarter than the other ones, because instead of slamming down and trying to hit him, it was sweeping its head in enormous arcs just above the snow.

It's going to hit me, Danny thought. He could not muster any real enthusiasm about this. He was too cold. He was vaguely aware that being hit by the iceworm would be bad, but couldn't seem to remember why that was.

A snowball flew past him and hit the side of the worm's head.

Whooping and shouting, Wendell and Christiana charged out of the rocks. Snowballs flew.

"Take that for trying to squish my friends!" cried Wendell.

Christiana flung snowballs with deadly precision, one in each hand.

TAKE THAT! TAKE THAT FOR BEING SCIENTIFICALLY IMPROBABLE!

The worm shook its head, apparently confused. Danny covered the last few yards to the rocks.

"Come on!" said Wendell, abandoning the snowballs. "There's a nest in here, and it's warm!"

"Oh good," said Danny weakly. "I'm very cold."

"Take that!" he heard Christiana say behind him. "Take that for not eating algae like a proper iceworm!"

Wendell led him to the edge of the nest. It was a shallow bowl made of rock, larger than Danny's bedroom. In the center lay a single gigantic egg.

"That's nice," said Danny, and fainted dead away.

HATCHED

He came to a minute later, with Wendell pouring tea down his throat.

"You're not dead until you're warm and dead," muttered the iguana. "Come on, Danny . . ."

Danny sputtered and sat up. "I'll be warm and *drowned* if you're not careful!"

Wendell let out a long sigh of relief and handed over the thermos.

Danny gulped down the fireweed tea. Heat spread through his body, and the coldness in his chest eased again.

"I was afraid you were a goner," said Wendell. "You turned *blue* that time."

"Neat!" said Danny. "Like a chameleon!"

NO, LIKE A POPSICLE.

Danny looked over at the egg. "Are there any eggshells?"

Wendell shook his head. "Only the egg.

"I guess we could break the egg," said Wendell slowly, "but I don't think that'd be good for the baby phoenix."

Danny sighed. He wanted to breathe fire again, preferably before he froze to death, but there was no way he was going to hurt a baby phoenix to get the eggshell. Particularly not after the adult phoenix had saved his life.

Christiana came up to the edge of the nest, put her feet over, and slid down the rock. "The iceworms are *really* worked up," she said. "I don't think they can tunnel through rock, but they're whacking themselves against the stones around this spot."

As she spoke, a loud thud emphasized her words, followed by the pained roaring of the worms.

"Why do you think they're so mad?" asked Wendell. "Or are they just hungry?"

"Maybe they were asleep," said Danny. "I get pretty grumpy when somebody wakes me up in the middle of the night." (*Thud . . . thud . . . thud . . . roar . . .*)

"Well, it is night," said Christiana. "Like . . . *Arctic* night. Which lasts for months."

"I wonder if there's a relationship," said Wendell. "The longer the night, the grumpier you are when you wake up in the middle of it. So if night lasts for six months—"

THEY'D BE *REALLY* GRUMPY!

AND THAT'S A LOT OF WORM TO BE GRUMPY TOO . . .

"I bet we could write an equation," said Wendell. (*Thud . . . roar . . . thud . . .*) "If X equals grumpiness and Y is the length of the night—"

Danny was saved from the horrors of algebra by a loud crackling noise.

"That didn't sound like a worm!"

"I think it's the egg!" said Danny.

All three of them spun to look at it.

It was rocking back and forth. As they watched, it gave another loud crack, and a zigzag ran down the side.

"Yes!" said Danny, pumping his fist in the air. "It's gonna hatch!"

This was a great relief. He'd been afraid that

they'd be sitting around waiting for the egg to hatch for hours. Or days.

His dad would undoubtedly notice if he was gone for days.

There was another crack, and another—and a great *whumph!* noise and suddenly they were covered in snow.

"Ack!" cried Wendell.

"What was that?" shouted Danny.

The snow melted as soon as it touched the warm rock. A few chunks landed on the egg itself and hissed away into steam.

"It's not snowing," said Christiana, wiping snow off her face.

IT DOESN'T NORMALLY SNOW IN CHUNKS.

Another pile of snow rolled over the top of the rocks.

The trio made their way to the opening in the rocks and looked out.

"What's it doing?" asked Danny.

The iceworm was rolling around in the snow, like a dog with an itchy spot on its back. It wiggled from side to side, throwing chunks high in the air.

"I think it's trying to cool off," said Christiana. "It got burned, so it was rolling around in snow, and threw some of it over the rocks."

Danny had a hard time feeling sorry for a creature that had tried to eat him, but it was a relief to know that the worm wasn't trying to get at them.

The worm shook itself off, then began slithering away across the snow. Danny stepped back into the safety of the rocks.

He was about to say something else—he wasn't entirely sure what—when there was a final, savage crack and the giant egg split in half.

SPARKS AND EGGSHELLS

Danny's first thought was that baby phoenixes were incredibly ugly.

The egg had been beautiful, glowing like alabaster. The adult phoenix was beautiful, like a bird of prey wreathed in flames.

The baby phoenix looked like a fat, soggy chicken.

It sat amid the wreckage of the eggshells with its eyes tightly closed. Its feathers were soaking wet and scraggly and the melted snow from the iceworm meant that it was sitting on its tail feathers in a puddle.

It opened its beak and cried.

SQUONK!

"Wow," said Christiana. "Just . . . *wow.*"

"Do you think it's supposed to look like that?" asked Danny.

"I don't think *anything's* supposed to look like that."

"SQUONK!" cried the chick again.

The phoenix swept in from overhead, calling angrily. Its voice sounded like fiery bells, like the crackle of flames, like the hiss of steam.

It did not sound like "Squonk."

For a moment, it looked as if the phoenix would land, and the kids backed away from the infant phoenix to avoid being burned. But all the snow that had landed among the rocks began to melt in the heat of the great bird's wings. The bowl was suddenly ankle deep in cold water.

The phoenix cried out in frustration and launched into the air.

Its wings trailed across the chick's feathers. The top of the baby phoenix's head caught fire—not like it was burning, but like the phoenix itself, a white crest of flame.

For a moment it looked as if the baby would catch fire like its parent—and then the melting snow doused the flame. The chick's crest guttered and went out.

"Squonk . . ." said the chick plaintively. The water was up to its wings and it was starting to shiver.

Danny could see the adult phoenix's problem. If it stayed to protect the chick, it would melt the snow and the chick would drown. If it left, the chick wouldn't catch fire the way phoenixes were supposed to do.

S-S-QUON-K-K . . .

"We have to save it!" said Danny. "It's getting cold!"

"And get you some eggshells," added Wendell.

"Right, that too."

They splashed down to the chick. It was about a third the size of Wendell and didn't look heavy, it just looked slimy.

The chick was trying to climb atop one of the eggshells. Danny put out his hand to the eggshell and found it still radiating heat, like bread fresh from the oven.

"Do we just grab it?" asked Wendell worriedly. "I don't want to get burned."

Christiana scowled and held out her hand over the chick's feathers. "It doesn't *feel* hot . . ."

Snow poured into the nest, turning the puddle into a slushy mess. Danny took a deep breath, reached out, and grabbed the phoenix chick.

It wasn't hot. It was cold, actually, and very soggy. The front of Danny's shirt was suddenly slimy with water and egg white.

SQUONK?

"Let's get out of here," said Danny. "Before we all freeze to death."

"There's some higher ground over there," said Christiana, pointing. "We'll be out of the water, anyhow."

The chick curled into Danny's chest and shivered.

They sloshed through the water. Danny wanted another gulp of fireweed tea, but the chick took both hands to carry and he couldn't get to the thermos. He wasn't sure if the coldness he was feeling was his fire going out, or the fact that he was clutching twenty pounds of soggy baby bird.

The wind slithered through chinks in the stone and chilled his wet feet.

At the top of the stone bowl, where two tall fingers of stone leaned together, there was a small cave. It was barely deep enough for all of them to fit, but it was out of the water and the wind.

Danny set the baby phoenix down and drank tea. The coldness retreated again, but not quite

as far. He hoped the effect wasn't wearing off. It would be really inconvenient to freeze right now.

Christiana was shivering. Danny handed her the thermos and she took a sip.

"Wendell should drink some too," said Danny, and then—"Wait, where's Wendell?"

"I'm right here," panted the iguana. He came up from the bowl, carrying one of the eggshells. "You forgot this."

"You're the best, Wendell."

Danny snapped off a chunk of eggshell. When it broke, sparks flashed and it smelled like burning.

It was a little weird to eat something that he'd

just watch something get born from, but . . . well . . .

He took a bite.

It was crunchy and tasted like cinnamon. Some of the shell fragments were rather sharp, so he had to chew carefully.

BE CAREFUL. IT MIGHT HAVE SALMONELLA. RAW EGGS CAN CARRY SALMONELLA SOMETIMES.

"I think phoenix eggs are cooked sort of by definition," said Christiana.

Danny bit off another chunk of eggshell. When he swallowed, the cold spot inside his chest began to feel strangely warm.

"Squonk!" said the chick miserably. Christiana took off her jacket and began rubbing the chick down with it. When she finished, it looked twice as miserable and its fluff stood up in all directions.

"What do we do?" asked Wendell. "I'm afraid it's going to freeze to death."

"It's supposed to be on fire," said Danny. "I'm sure of it. The phoenix tried to set it on fire, but then it was wet, so it didn't take."

"Can you breathe fire on it? Is the eggshell working?"

Danny rubbed his sternum. Underneath it, he could feel things shifting and fizzing, sort of like when he drank a soda too fast and had to burp.

He tried breathing fire. Oily, cinnamon-scented smoke poured out of his mouth, but that was all.

GAH! DO THAT OUTSIDE!

"It's not there yet," said Danny. He broke off another chunk of eggshell and sparks flashed around the interior of the cave.

"Can we light it on fire with those?" asked Christiana.

"Good question . . ."

Danny hunched over the chick and broke the eggshell into smaller pieces. Bright fragments of light landed on the chick, and for a moment he was hopeful, but they fizzled out.

He shook his head. "It's not lasting long enough," he said. He ate the eggshell bits and belched. More smoke came out. Christiana scowled.

The chick fell on its side, as if it didn't have the strength to sit up any longer. Its chest moved shallowly.

"Do something!" said Wendell frantically. "It's dying! Danny—!"

"What am I supposed to do?!" said Danny. "I'm a dragon! I'm not a phoenix or a veterinarian!" He looked around and grabbed the thermos of fireweed tea. "Maybe if it drinks a little of this . . ."

Wendell held the chick's head while Danny dribbled a few drops into its beak. The baby phoenix did not resist. After a moment, it chirped.

"That's helping!" said Wendell. "Give it more!"
"There's hardly any left," said Danny.

THEN GIVE
IT THE REST!
WE CAN'T LET IT
FREEZE!

Danny looked at Christiana. She looked from him to the chick and back. Then she sighed.

"Do it," she said. "I mean, we *shouldn't,* because we'll probably die, but that's gonna be hours from now and the chick's gonna freeze *right now.*"

Danny nodded. "As long as we all agree," he said, and poured the rest of the fireweed tea down the phoenix's throat.

HERBERT

The chick spluttered. For a long minute, Danny was afraid that it had been too little too late, and he'd just doomed them all for nothing —or worse, that he'd doomed them all and drowned the chick in the process.

Then it swallowed. And a moment later, it sighed happily and emitted a tiny burp.

Wendell's breath went out in a whoosh and he wrapped his arms around the baby phoenix.

"Now what?" asked Christiana. She poked her head out of the front of the cave. "The phoenix is still gone . . ."

The distant roars of iceworms echoed through the stone. The nest-bowl was waist-deep in slush. Danny wasn't looking forward to wading through it.

"We need to get out of here," he said. "I've eaten the eggshell, and it's definitely doing something, so I guess we can just go home."

"We can't go yet," said Wendell firmly.
"What?" said Danny. "Why not?"
"We can't leave Herbert," said Wendell.

HERBERT?!

"He looks like a Herbert," said Wendell. "And we can't leave him until he's on fire like a proper phoenix should be. What if the tea wears off while we're gone?"

Danny wasn't used to Wendell sounding so confident. He looked at Christiana, who shrugged helplessly.

"Don't look at me, he's the one who named it."

"But how are we going to set him on fire?" asked Danny. "We don't have anything that burns! I can't breathe fire!" (Actually, he thought he was getting heartburn. His innards were definitely roiling now.)

"We could set a backpack on fire," said Wendell. "Or our clothes . . ."

"Clothes are surprisingly hard to set on fire," said Danny.

LOOK, STUFF HAPPENS, OKAY? IT'S NOT LIKE ANYBODY DIED!

THE FIREFIGHTERS WERE AWFULLY SARCASTIC ABOUT IT, THOUGH . . .

"If you were only a trifle more competent, you'd be a juvenile delinquent," said Christiana.

"So's your m—*grandmother.*"

"I'm not leaving Herbert," said Wendell stubbornly. "You two go on without me if you want."

Christiana rolled her eyes. "Like we're going to do *that.*"

They sat glumly in the cave, listening to the roar of the worms. Danny tried to breathe fire again and thought for a second that he was going to throw up. He clamped both hands over his snout and his eyes streamed.

Wendell reached into his backpack and squirted hand sanitizer onto his hands. When Danny raised his eyebrow, he said "What? I'm not leaving Herbert, but I don't want to get . . . I dunno, firebird flu or something."

Christiana suddenly sat bolt upright. "That's it!" she said.

"Firebird flu?" asked Wendell.

"No!" She snatched the bottle away from him and waved it in the air.

"Hey, I need that!"

"Herbert needs it more," she said.

DON'T YOU KNOW? *HAND SANITIZER BURNS!*

MAMA WENDELL

"If my mom ever finds out that I am playing with fire, I will be grounded," said Wendell. "And then shot. And then grounded again."

"Very sensible," said Christiana. "A lot of wildfires are started by kids being stupid and then the next thing you know, half the world's burning down. But I think when you're surrounded on all sides by snow, it's not quite the same. I mean, what are we gonna burn out here?"

"Ourselves," said Wendell glumly.

"That's why Danny's gonna do it."

"Hey!" said Danny, who wasn't sure if this meant that he was the most competent person or just that Christiana didn't care if he got burned.

"Look, you're a dragon," said Christiana. "You're more fireproof than the rest of us, at least a little."

ALL THOSE TIMES YOU DIDN'T BELIEVE I WAS A DRAGON, AND NOW THAT YOU KNOW I AM, I'M NOT SURE I LIKE IT . . .

"I'm worried about this," said Wendell. "What if phoenix fire isn't like regular fire and we hurt Herbert?"

"We'll douse my jacket," said Christiana, "and set it on fire with the sparks from the eggshell.

If it's some special kind of fire, then the eggshell should do it, right? And then if Herbert wants to get close to it, we let him, and if he doesn't, we won't have lost anything. Except my jacket."

"And my hope of not contracting a horrible disease on this trip," said Wendell.

"One of these days, we've got to talk about this recreational hypochondria of yours, Wendell. It's not healthy."

"The what?" asked Danny.

"He thinks he's sick for fun," whispered Christiana.

"Do not . . ." muttered Wendell.

After a moment, the iguana sighed. "Okay," he said. "We'll try it. But if it looks like Herbert might get burned, we're stopping, okay?"

"Instantly," said Danny.

"Faster than you can say 'hypochondria,'" said Christiana.

"It better be a lot faster than that," said Wendell, scowling.

Christiana laid out her jacket and Danny pumped hand sanitizer onto it until the bottle made empty splorching sounds.

"It'll be okay," Wendell told Herbert. "You don't have to go near the fire if you don't want to."

But the instant Danny cracked the eggshell, it became obvious that Herbert wanted to very much.

Sparks landed on the jacket and it blazed up so fast that Danny jumped back. The fire was electric white, the color of phoenix feathers. The air smelled sharp and acrid.

Herbert rolled out of Wendell's arms and lunged toward the flame.

"Herbert!" said Wendell. "Wait! It's not your mom, it's a jacket—"

SQUON-N-NK!

The baby phoenix dove into the white flame. All three reptiles held their breath, at first from anticipation and then because the cave was filling up with smoke.

"Gah!" said Christiana. Wendell began to cough.

They couldn't see Herbert anymore. All they could see was roiling smoke.

Danny grabbed them both by the arm and pulled them out of the cave.

BUT—COUGH—COUGH—HERBERT—COUGH—WE HAVE TO—COUGH—GO BACK—

"You'll suffocate!" said Christiana. "Jeez! How did one jacket make that much smoke?"

"But Herbert—!"

And then from the cave came a crackling sound and a roar and a blaze of light—

The baby phoenix came out of the cave. He was still covered in down and looked a bit unfinished, but his eyes were open and white fire poured off him. The smoke coming out of the cave made a stark black backdrop.

He spread his wings. They didn't look big enough to fly yet.

He flapped once or twice, thoughtfully.

Then he folded his wings and stomped determinedly toward Wendell.

"Herbert!" said Wendell happily. "You did it! It was the right kind of fire after all!"

The chick walked up to Wendell, and before the iguana could get out of the way, leaned against him.

"Wendell!" said Danny, expecting the iguana to catch fire himself.

Herbert gazed adoringly up at Wendell.

"Who's a good phoenix, then? Are *you* a good phoenix? Are you the best little phoenix ever?" Wendell scratched Herbert's crest and the chick chirped happily and closed his eyes.

"Well, I'm gonna be sick," said Christiana.

"Okay," said Danny. "Herbert's fine, he's on fire like a phoenix should be, I ate the eggshell, so let's go home now." (He actually wanted to go lie down for a while. His stomach felt very weird and wiggly. Apparently getting your fire restarted was not a pleasant process.)

"Right," said Wendell. "Herbert, you be a good phoenix and stay here. Your mom—or dad, or whatever—will be along shortly." He patted the little phoenix's head. "And you grow up to be a great big phoenix and maybe I'll be able to come back and see you someday, okay?"

The trio walked away, along the rim of the bowl. Herbert looked puzzled, then fell into step behind Wendell.

"No," said Wendell. "You have to stay here. Stay. *Stay.*"

He backed away, holding up his hands. Herbert blinked a few times.

"That's right," said Wendell. "Stay . . . stay . . . good phoenix . . ."

Herbert's beak opened. The chick struggled for a moment, and then . . .

BABY PHOENIX LIZARD

"Oh crud," said Christiana. "They talk! The big one didn't talk!"

"Well, it didn't really get a chance," Danny admitted. "I mean, it was all in and out and fight iceworms and back . . ."

"Mama!" said Herbert again, and waddled up to Wendell.

"But I'm not your mama!" said Wendell.

Herbert sat on his foot.

"I think he imprinted on you," said Christiana. "Some baby birds do that—the first thing that moves, it sees and thinks that's its mom."

PROFESSOR WENDELL'S GUIDE TO BIRD IMPRINTING

WHEN SOME BABY BIRDS HATCH, THEY IMPRINT ON THE FIRST THING THEY SEE. THEY BELIEVE THAT IT'S THEIR MOM, AND THEREFORE, THEY MUST BE . . . WHATEVER THEIR MOM IS TOO.

I'M A BIRD!

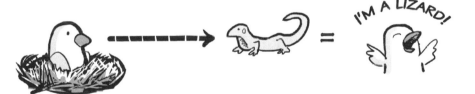

I'M A LIZARD!

I'M A ROCK!

"So do something!" said Danny. "Imprint Herbert on something else!"

"It doesn't work like that," said Christiana. "They fixate on one particular thing. When people are raising super-endangered birds to release in the wild, they have to feed them with hand-puppets that look like the adult birds, or the baby will think it's a person."

She considered this. "I suppose we should probably have had some kind of burning phoenix hand puppet for Herbert . . ."

"Mama!" said Herbert happily, gazing up at Wendell.

". . . We're doomed," said Danny, covering his eyes.

Because his eyes were covered, he missed the phoenix landing in the stone bowl. All he heard was a whoosh of wings.

"What have you done?" cried the adult phoenix, in a voice like shattered bells. *"What have you done?"*

Under the phoenix, the ice water began to bubble.

"Somehow I don't think we have to worry about freezing to death anymore . . ." said Christiana under her breath.

"No, we're going to get *roasted,*" Danny whispered back.

I SAVED YOU OUT OF THE *GOODNESS* OF MY HEART, AND *THIS* IS HOW YOU REPAY ME?

"I'm sorry!" cried Wendell. "I didn't mean to—I mean— he was going to freeze, and we had to get his fires going, but I didn't expect him to—"

I'M SORRY!

"We didn't mean to wake the iceworms," Christiana piped up. "We didn't know they were under the snow like that, or we wouldn't have walked on them."

The phoenix swung her great head around and looked down at Christiana instead of Wendell. Christiana took a step back, but faced the giant bird squarely.

"Your body heat woke them," she said. "They are creatures of cold. Even your meager warmth burned them like fire."

"They must hate you, then," said Danny. "You're all fiery."

"We are ancient enemies," said the phoenix.

"But this time of year they sleep. They would not have come so close to my nest if they were not enraged."

"Sorry!" said the phoenix. "Yes, we are all sorry! But that does not change the fact that a child of immortal fire has imprinted on a . . . a *lizard.*"

She said "lizard" so scornfully and Wendell looked so miserable that Danny had to speak up.

HEY, IF IT WASN'T FOR THAT LIZARD, HERBERT WOULD HAVE FROZEN TO DEATH!

The phoenix stared at him. Her eyes swirled with flame and seemed to burn as they bored into Danny. Danny gritted his teeth, but refused to look away. He was a dragon! A dragon was just as good as a phoenix! And Wendell was his best friend! No giant burning bird talked about his friends like that!

"Wendell saved your chick's life!" he shouted, and then nearly doubled over. His innards were *really* gurgling now. It sounded like a washing machine was starting up under his rib cage.

"*Herbert?*" said the phoenix.

"He looked like a Herbert," said Wendell weakly.

The phoenix stood before them, looking tall and fiery and elegant, and then she let out a long, blistering sigh and put her wing over her face.

... I GOTTA SIT DOWN.

FIERY PUKE

The phoenix sat in the water, which began to steam gently. The three kids sat down on the edge of the bowl and put their feet in the water. It was as hot as a bathtub. Christiana sighed happily.

Herbert curled up next to Wendell and gazed adoringly into the iguana's glasses.

The phoenix looked at the two of them and shook her head. "I don't know," she said wearily. "You spend all eternity living and burning and rising from the ashes and then life throws you a curve."

"Maybe if I leave, Herbert will forget about me?" said Wendell hopefully.

OUR LIFE SPANS ARE MEASURED IN MILLENNIA. HERBERT WILL REMEMBER YOU LONG AFTER YOU'VE DIED OF OLD AGE.

The phoenix grimaced. "*Herbert.* Bleh."

"What do phoenixes usually call themselves?" asked Christiana.

"Names with majesty," said the phoenix. "I am called Sun-Blazing-on-the-Snows-Eternal. My brother was called Dancing-in-the-Heart-of-the-Farthest-Star."

"Hoo," said Danny. "I bet it takes forever to write your name on the top of your papers in school."

"You may call me Sun-Blazing," said the phoenix. She scowled. "I was going to name him Aurora-Burning-on-the-Highest-Mountain, but I suppose he's Herbert now."

Privately Danny thought that Herbert looked much more like a Herbert than an Aurora-Burning-on-the-Highest-Mountain. It did not seem like a good time to mention this.

He opened his mouth to say something and then his stomach clenched, almost like it did when he was about to throw up.

"Danny?" said Wendell. "Are you okay?"

Danny leaped to his feet and ran to the edge of the stone bowl.

He opened his mouth, expecting to throw up—
and barfed fire.

It was *horrible*.

Being a dragon, his throat was fairly well
insulated against breathing fire, but his stomach
wasn't. He suddenly understood what *heartburn*
was, and why there were so many commercials
on TV advertising cures for it.

"You're breathing fire!" cried Wendell, delighted.

"No, I'm not," croaked Danny. He grabbed a
handful of snow and tried to wash his mouth out
with it. "I'm *puking* fire. It's the worst thing ever."

He coughed up more fire and clutched his chest.

> **WORSE THAN THE TIME BIG EDDY TRIED TO FLUSH YOUR HEAD DOWN THE TOILET IN THE BOYS' BATHROOM?**

"Worse," said Danny. "Much worse."

The fire was dark and sort of drippy. It pattered over the snow and melted through it like acid.

"Great-Granddad didn't warn me about this . . ." moaned Danny.

"Ew," said Christiana, coming up beside him.

The phoenix landed next to them. "I'm sorry you're not feeling well," she said, "but your fire is attracting attention."

Danny looked up blearily.

All around the edge of the snowfield, he could see white shapes heaving themselves over the snow.

The iceworms were returning.

And they had brought reinforcements.

GLOW WORMS

"So that's a lot of worms," said Christiana. "Um. *Quite* a lot."

She stood beside (and slightly behind) Danny, staying out of the line of fire.

"Bleerraggh . . ." said Danny. His mouth tasted like the bottom of a charcoal grill.

The phoenix shook her head slowly. "I've never seen so many," she said. "You must have woken half the population."

"Sorry," said Wendell. "We didn't mean to . . ."

The giant bird rolled her eyes. "You've gotten my chick to imprint on you and brought a horde of giant iceworms to attack my nest site. I'd hate to see what would happen if you *did* mean to do something."

Danny wanted to say something in their defense, but he was afraid if he opened his mouth, more fire was going to come up.

"So maybe now would be a good time to retreat," said Christiana.

"Good luck with that," said the phoenix. "This is the only really defensible place for miles. That's why I put my nest in it." She frowned. "Normally the iceworms sleep until summer, and then they migrate away. They never bother me. Then again, I also don't land on their roosting grounds when they're trying to sleep."

"Sorry," said Wendell, for approximately the hundredth time.

Christiana and Wendell each took one of Danny's arms and hauled him back into the relative safety of the rocks.

"I am going to try to draw them off," said the phoenix. "Don't leave. And don't let Herbert get hurt."

Wendell let go of Danny and wrapped his arms around Herbert. The phoenix chick chirped happily.

The adult phoenix sighed and spread her wings.

From the edge of the stone bowl, they watched as she dove at the approaching iceworms. Their blunt heads turned to follow her. She banked sideways, leading them away, and a large number gave chase.

"I think it's working!" said Wendell.

"Not quite," said Christiana. "Look, there's still a couple coming this way . . ."

"Bleagh," said Danny. He peered blearily into the snow.

And indeed, it looked like Christiana was right. The bulk of the iceworms were following the phoenix, but a few determined individuals were approaching the stone nest.

"It'll be fine," said Wendell. "We'll just wait in here like before, and they'll get tired and go away."

SOMEHOW I DON'T THINK IT'S GOING TO BE THAT EASY . . .

The iceworms reached the rocky outcropping and paused. Two of them swung their heads back and forth in front of the stone.

The third crawled up beside them and all three began swaying in unison.

"Thaaaaat's weird," said Danny.

The worms began to make a strange, high keening noise.

"Uh," said Wendell. "Are the things on their heads . . . glowing?"

It was hard to tell, in the blinding white of the snow, but there seemed to be a faint glow coming from the green patches on their heads.

"Not gonna lie," said Christiana. "That's starting to creep me out. I don't think tiny iceworms do that."

"I think . . . I think they're talking . . ." said Wendell.

"To us?" said Danny.

Wendell shook his head. "To *each other*."

"Yay," said Christiana. "Telepathic glowing iceworms. Next time you get sick, Danny, go to the emergency room like everybody else."

The iceworms moved.

One oozed forward and lay down against the

rock. A white wall of flesh covered the entrance to the bowl.

"And we're trapped," said Christiana.

Wendell hugged Herbert more tightly. "It'll be okay," he told the chick.

Danny wondered if he'd be able to breathe fire. Surely the horrible fire in his stomach must be close to igniting his internal furnaces by now!

He tried to breathe fire, discreetly, and retched again.

UNGHGHGHH. . . .

"What are they doing out there?" asked Wendell.

Christiana shook her head. They could hear the sounds of the iceworms dragging against the stone. The strange sloughing noise echoed through the stone bowl.

"They're circling," said Christiana. "Are they trying to find a way in?"

An enormous green head appeared over the top of the stones.

Danny wiped his mouth with the back of his hand. "Isn't it obvious?" he asked, when he was sure he could speak again. "They're *climbing*."

WORM TEAMWORK

"Worms can't climb," said Wendell. "I mean, not very far, anyway. Can they?"

"They don't have to climb very far," said Christiana grimly. "Danny's right." She turned, following the sounds of wormflesh scraping against the stones. "One wrapped around and another climbed on top of it. If the third one climbs on top of it . . ." She shook her head. "That's what they were talking to each other about. They had to make a plan. I can't believe they were smart enough for that . . ."

"Maybe they're smarter together," said Wendell. "Like a hive mind."

"Oh, that's a happy thought."

Christiana turned to Danny. "Can you breathe fire yet?"

Danny shook his head.

IT'S NOT THAT I DON'T WANT TO. IT'S JUST THAT I KEEP BARFING WHEN I TRY.

ALL RIGHT, CAN YOU BARF FIRE, THEN?

Danny felt horrible.
Wendell didn't sound much better.

Danny put a hand over his stomach. It felt awful and acidic, but it also felt . . . empty.

"Sorry," he said. "I think I already threw up everything."

Christiana nodded and turned sharply on her heel. She waded out into the water in the center of the stone bowl and knelt down.

"Uh . . . Christiana?"

He would have asked what she was doing, but at that moment, the head of an iceworm came over the top of the stones.

"If we get in the warm water, they won't be able to pick us out, right?" said Danny. "If they're attracted to heat?"

Wendell peered up at the iceworm. "Maybe?" he said.

The iceworm began to slide over the stones, down into the bowl. Rock dust drifted down around them. The nest, which had seemed quite large before, suddenly got a lot smaller.

"Or we could go hide in the cave," said Danny. "Let's do that."

Wendell picked up Herbert. Christiana was still rooting around in the water.

They backed toward the cave. Danny wasn't sure what they were going to do once they got there, but it was bound to be better than being squished.

"Christiana!" he called. "Uh, Christiana . . . ?"

I SEE IT!

The end of the worm touched the water. It recoiled as if burned.

"Maybe it'll be too warm!" said Wendell hopefully.

The worm shook itself. It pulled back from the water and began sliding down, along the edge of the nest, avoiding the water.

". . . or not," said Danny.

"Maybe the phoenix will come back?" said Wendell, somewhat less hopefully.

Christiana stood up and sprinted for the cave.

The motion must have attracted the iceworm. It turned its great head toward her, snuffling at the air. Ripples of water touched its side as it moved and it shuddered, but did not retreat.

"It's getting used to the water . . ." said Wendell.

"That's bad," said Danny.

Christiana paused. The iceworm's head lay between her and the cave, moving back and forth.

Its head began to glow again. It suddenly lifted up a few feet and seemed to fix on Christiana.

The worm swung its head toward Danny.

"Hey, look, it worked!" said Danny. "Worm! Your mama is so worm-like she . . . um . . . slithers . . . I'm not good at ending these . . ."

"It's not responding to the jokes," snapped Christiana, splashing toward the cave. "It's responding to the motion— *Look out!*"

The iceworm's head slammed down, inches from Danny. He jumped back, into the cave.

It reared back and began sniffing along itself, looking for squashed dragon again. That was all the opening Christiana needed to run forward, through the gap, and into the cave herself.

It was dark inside, stained with smoke, but the worm couldn't possibly fit through the opening.

"You made it!" Wendell said. Christiana panted.

Outside the cave, the iceworm discovered that it had not squashed anyone and roared in displeasure.

"We're safe in here, right?" said Wendell. "It can't possibly fit—"

The cave went very dark. The only light came from Herbert's fiery feathers.

"I'm not sure it knows that," said Danny.

FIRE AND BURPS

The iceworm pressed forward, filling the mouth of the cave. It met resistance and retreated slightly.

The expression on a giant eyeless worm face was hard to read, but Danny thought that it looked frustrated.

It jammed itself forward again. Its body squished and flexed and it made it another few inches into the cave.

"Safe?" said Christiana. "Err. I don't think we're that safe. If it's like a big earthworm, it can expand and contract itself pretty well . . ."

BARF ON IT, DANNY!

I CAN'T! MY STOMACH'S TOTALLY EMPTY! I PRACTICALLY THREW UP MY TOENAILS!

Danny couldn't even *remember* food.

"Mama!" said Herbert, hiding behind Wendell. The chick chirped miserably.

"Do something!" said Wendell. "It's scaring Herbert!"

"Forget Herbert, it's scaring *me!*" said Christiana as the worm forced its way slowly through the passage.

Its head was glowing again. The cave was filled with ghastly worm-light. Small rocks fell from the ceiling. The expression (and Danny still wasn't sure if he was imagining it) grew focused and intent.

It squished forward another foot. Danny could see its skin flexing against the stone.

"Right," muttered Christiana. She pressed something hard and cinnamon-scented into Danny's hand. "Here, eat this."

Danny had to hold it up in front of him, blinking by the dim light of the worm's head and Herbert's flames.

IS THIS MORE PHOENIX EGGSHELL?

WELL, I DIDN'T PACK ANY GRANOLA BARS.

"I dunno," said Danny. The thought of eating more eggshell made his stomach roil again. "Just the thought is pretty nauseating . . ."

"How's the thought of getting eaten alive by gigantic annelids treating you?" asked Christiana.

"What's an annelid?"

"It's another word for *worm,*" said Wendell, "and I never thought I'd say this, but maybe this isn't the best time for a vocabulary lesson?"

The worm got another few inches into the cave. It bit at the air, insomuch as something without teeth could bite. Herbert wailed.

Danny shoved the eggshell into his mouth.

It was just as sickening as he thought it would be. The cinnamon taste had been pleasant at first, but mostly it reminded him of how sick he was going to be in a minute. He swallowed hard, feeling sharp bits of eggshell gouging his throat on the way down.

It would be really awful to choke to death on an eggshell right before being eaten by an iceworm. The worm roared. The sound, in the enclosed space, was deafening.

The sound knocked Wendell over. He landed on his back and his glasses went flying. Herbert chirped in confusion.

Danny's stomach felt like someone had kicked him with a boot covered in hot sauce.

"C'mon," said Christiana, watching him closely. "You can do it!"

"You're not—*urrp*—helping—" said Danny.

Speaking was a mistake—or the best thing he could have done, depending on your outlook. Danny's innards rebelled.

He barfed fire.

Christiana grabbed his shoulders and pointed him at the iceworm.

Something happened inside Danny's chest. It felt like a match being dragged along the rough strip on a matchbox.

Scrape . . . scrape . . .

FWOOOOOOM!

He actually felt his fire ignite. Suddenly flame poured out of his mouth—real, honest-to-goodness dragon fire, not the awful . . . whatever that was . . . that he'd been bringing up before.

The iceworm shrieked.

In fairness, almost anyone would shriek if you threw up on them, but dragon fire and dragon stomach acid together was a horrifyingly potent mix. The worm jerked backward, trying to escape, and yanked itself completely out of the hole.

"Go, Danny!" cried Christiana.

Danny staggered forward, flaming wildly. It wasn't that he didn't want the worm to escape, but now that he'd started breathing fire, he wasn't sure if he could stop. It felt like his whole torso was a thin skin filled with fire instead of bones.

The worm was retreating over the edge of the stones.

He remembered Great-Grandfather Dragon-breath telling him not to flame any of his friends when his fire reignited. At the time, he'd thought it was an odd thing to say, but now it made sense. He couldn't seem to stop breathing fire.

"Is it gone?" called Wendell from the cave. "I can't find my glasses . . ."

Herbert wandered out of the front of the cave, chirping worriedly.

There were too many people in the nest, and Danny didn't want to hit any of them. When he turned his head, fire shot out at an angle and left a black line of char across the stones.

He ran toward the entry to the stone bowl. The worm that had been blocking the way moved in a hurry when it felt fire come toward it. All Danny saw was the worm's retreating back.

He fell to his knees and tried to eat snow to douse the fire. Unfortunately it melted before he could get the snow to his mouth.

Behind him, he heard "There they are!" and "Mama!"

Danny took a deep, deep breath through his nose, gulped—

—held it—

—and let out a belch so loud that it echoed over the snow like the roar of an iceworm.

BRRRAAAAAAGHHHHHHH

The fire petered out.

"Eww," said Christiana behind him. "Excuse *you*."

Danny exhaled. It smelled like smoke, but it wasn't burning. His stomach felt much better.

"Fire's back," he said, and grinned.

LOVE AND GLASSES

The phoenix landed in the stone bowl, beating her wings until the surface of the water rippled with steam.

"Judging by the worm tracks outside, you've had some excitement," she said. "Is Herbert okay?"

"Mama," said Herbert cheerfully, leaning on Wendell. The phoenix sighed.

I'VE LED THE WORMS OFF. YOU CAN PROBABLY GET BACK ACROSS THE SNOWFIELD BEFORE THEY RETURN.

"Did you know that they communicate with each other?" demanded Christiana. "Their heads glowed and then they started working together!"

The phoenix stared at her. "Really," she said finally. "That's . . . unsettling."

"You're telling us!"

"I'll keep an eye out for that. Maybe the ice-worms are evolving. Maybe this isn't the best place for a nest site." The phoenix sighed. "And I still don't know what we're going to do about my chick."

"Maybe I could come see him after school . . ." said Wendell. The steam was fogging up his glasses, so he took them off to wipe them on his shirt.

Herbert let out a worried chirp. "Mama?"

"Eh?" said Wendell. "I'm right here . . ."

"Mama!" said Herbert, sounding agitated. The chick looked around.

Wendell put his glasses back on. Herbert let out a chirp of relief and wrapped his wings around Wendell's leg.

A memory teased at Danny. He'd barely been listening, he'd been so worried about not breathing fire, but he'd heard it anyway. Wendell had been looking for his glasses, and Herbert had been freaking out. At the time, he'd thought that it was fear of the worms, but . . .

"Wendell," he said, "take your glasses off for a minute, will you?"

"Okay . . ." said Wendell.

CHIRRRPP??

Christiana had the same thought at the same moment Danny did. She wheeled around and looked at the phoenix. "How good is your eyesight when you're a chick?"

The phoenix blinked. "Uh . . . not great . . . ? I mean, you don't have anything much to compare it to, but it gets better as we get older."

Danny took Wendell's glasses and put them on his nose. Herbert let out of a chirp of delight and waddled toward him.

"Mama!"

"He's not imprinted on you!" said Danny, delighted. The phoenix chick was extremely warm. It was like being hugged by a space heater. He took the glasses off and was relieved when Herbert let go of his leg. "He's not imprinted on *you,* Wendell, he's imprinted on your *glasses!*"

Wendell gulped.

"My mom is gonna kill me . . ." he said sadly. He took the glasses back and put them on his nose. Herbert gazed up at him adoringly.

"You be a good phoenix, Herbert," said the iguana. "You get big and strong and burny and be the best phoenix ever."

He scratched the chick behind the ruff and Herbert crooned happily.

Then he took off his glasses and handed them to Danny. Danny waded up to the phoenix and set them, very carefully, on the end of the giant bird's beak.

Herbert looked around, puzzled, then saw the phoenix. "Mama!" he chirped happily.

"I can't see a thing through these," grumbled the phoenix. "But if this is what we have to do . . ."

She extended a wing over her chick and he snuggled happily against her side.

After a minute she said, "You know, he does kind of look like a Herbert."

THE FIRE-BREATHING DRAGON GOES HOME

"I'm not crying," said Wendell as the trio walked across the snowfield. "I'm *not*."

"I never said you were," said Danny.

"Somebody's probably just cutting onions," said Christiana. "In . . . err . . . the Farthest North. Invisibly."

"That's probably it. Stupid invisible onions." Wendell wiped his eyes.

The trip back didn't seem to take as long, possibly because Danny was able to breathe fire. When patches of ice threatened, he exhaled on them and melted them away into nothingness.

On the downside, Wendell couldn't see, and so was holding on to Christiana's arm the entire way.

The iceworms had left great gouges and troughs and wallows in the surface of the snow. It no longer looked like the pristine white blanket that it had been before.

"Sort of looks like people have been driving on it," said Danny. "Only with, y'know, *giant* cars."

"Giant *wiggly* cars," said Christiana, leading Wendell through a long worm-shaped ravine in the snow.

"I wonder about the communicating, and the glowing," said the iguana, peering about near-sightedly. "How smart do you think they are?"

"I'm more worried that we'll have a snow day and they'll come rampaging out of the Farthest North," said Danny. "I mean, we'd get out of school, but . . ."

"I don't think we need to worry too much about monsters that can be defeated by luke-warm water," said Christiana.

But they were all glad to leave the iceworm preserve behind.

The bottomless chasm on the way back had been worrying Danny, but it proved easy. He just took a deep breath and breathed fire on it.

The snow boiled away into steam, revealing a long span of stone. Danny tested his footing and grinned.

"Bone dry," he said.

He went first, melting the snow in front of them. By the end, his throat was starting to get a little dry, but that was all.

When the wind pushed at them, all they had to do was set their feet and it howled harmlessly past.

"You're better than de-icer," said Christiana. "Don't worry, Wendell, it's like a sidewalk. Just follow me."

On the far side they paused. Christiana carefully hooked the sign back up on the rope. "Just in case somebody decides they want to go fishing," she said.

Their footprints had left a clear trail to follow back to the portal. Danny felt his internal fires burning brightly—more brightly than he could ever remember. His chest felt delightfully warm.

THIS IS AWESOME, GUYS! I MIGHT BE ABLE TO BREATHE FIRE WITHOUT HAVING TO STICK MY HEAD IN THE FREEZER NOW!

"I don't know how you'd tell," said Christiana. "We're standing in a giant walk-in freezer right now."

"I'll try when we get back to Great-Granddad's house," said Danny. He could feel things shifting around inside his chest. The fire felt hot and . . . *there,* somehow, like it never had before.

His parents were going to be so excited when they found out he could breathe fire!

He led the way across the snow.

When they reached the top of the hill, they looked back across the snowfield. It was still blindingly white, but it seemed smaller now that they had walked across it. Twice.

The portal hummed and swirled in the stone. Christiana put her hand through it and frowned.

"Problem?" asked Danny.

"Something . . . oh, for Pete's sake." She rolled her eyes. "Your granddad closed the refrigerator door."

She pulled her hand back out, holding a bottle of ketchup.

Danny laughed. He reached through the portal and thumped on the inside of the fridge. After a minute, they could hear Great-Grandfather Dragonbreath yelling, "Hold your horses! I'm coming!"

Danny walked to the edge of the ledge and gazed out. The stars glittered like tiny points of fire against the ice.

The Farthest North was awfully pretty. And if you were a dragon and could breathe fire, it wasn't a bad place at all.

"Maybe we can come back someday and see how Herbert's doing," said Wendell.

"If we do, I'm packing a sweater," said Christiana.

"Think of the adventures we can have now that I can breathe fire!" said Danny.

"Oh goodie. I always wanted to see the inside of a burn ward . . ." muttered Wendell.

The portal creaked. "You there, Wanda? Did you get my grandson patched up, or is he a dragon-sicle?"

"He's fine, sir!" called Wendell.

"Let's go," said Christiana. "I'm starting to get cold."

"And I have to go find my old pair of glasses," said Wendell.

Danny nodded.

He was the last one through the portal, and he couldn't resist taking one last look over his shoulder.

The sky was black and the snow was white. For just a moment, Danny thought he saw a streak of light that might have been the aurora, or the tail of the phoenix flying across the horizon.

It had been a grand adventure. And Danny had no doubts that he'd have many more. But the nice thing about adventures was going home afterward.

He breathed a little fire—just a little, enough to crackle through the air—and turned and went through the portal, going home.

URSULA VERNON

is the award-winning creator of the
Dragonbreath and Hamster Princess series, as
well as *Castle Hangnail*. She lives, draws, and
stays warm in Pittsboro, North Carolina.

URSULAVERNON.COM